My Little Bear
A Treasury of Bear Tales
This edition produced 2007 for
BOOKS ARE FUN LTD
1680 Hwy 1 North, Fairfield, Iowa, IA 52556
by LITTLE TIGER PRESS
An imprint of Magi Publications
1 The Coda Centre, 189 Munster Road,
London SW6 6AW, UK
www.littletigerpress.com
This volume copyright © Magi Publications 2005
All rights reserved
ISBN 978-1-84506-645-1
Printed in China
10 9 8 7 6 5 4 3 2 1

Beware of the Bears!
Alan MacDonald
Illustrated by Gwyneth Williamson
First published in Great Britain 1998
by Little Tiger Press,
an imprint of Magi Publications
Text copyright © Alan MacDonald 1998
Illustrations copyright © Gwyneth Williamson 1998

Where There's a Bear, There's Trouble!
Michael Catchpool
Illustrated by Vanessa Cabban
First published in Great Britain 2002
by Little Tiger Press,
an imprint of Magi Publications
Text copyright © Michael Catchpool 2002
Illustrations copyright © Vanessa Cabban 2002

Who's Been Eating My Porridge?
M. Christina Butler
Illustrated by Daniel Howarth
First published in Great Britain 2004
by Little Tiger Press,
an imprint of Magi Publications
Text copyright © M. Christina Butler 2004
Illustrations copyright © Daniel Howarth 2004

Big Bear Little Bear
David Bedford
Illustrated by Jane Chapman
First published in Great Britain 2001
by Little Tiger Press,
an imprint of Magi Publications
Text copyright © David Bedford 2001
Illustrations copyright © Jane Chapman 2001

When will it be Spring?
Catherine Walters
First published in Great Britain 1997
by Little Tiger Press,
an imprint of Magi Publications
Text and illustrations copyright © Catherine Walters 1997

I'll Always Love You
Paeony Lewis
Illustrated by Penny Ives
First published in Great Britain 2000
by Little Tiger Press,
an imprint of Magi Publications
Text copyright © Paeony Lewis 2000
Illustrations copyright © Penny Ives 2000

My Little Bear
A Treasury of Bear Tales

Little Tiger Press

BEWARE of the BEARS!

by Alan MacDonald

pictures by Gwyneth Williamson

When the three bears saw what Goldilocks had done to their little cottage, they were hopping mad.

Their porridge eaten!

Chairs broken!

Beds bounced on!

"Go after her! Find out where she lives!" ordered Daddy Bear.

Baby Bear jumped on his scooter
and sped after Goldilocks.

In no time at all he was back.

"She lives on the far side of the forest," panted Baby Bear. "And what's more, she's just gone out and left her door unlocked."

"Good!" said Mommy Bear. "What are we waiting for? Let's see how *she* likes having uninvited guests."

Baby Bear led the way through the forest to Goldilocks's cottage. The door was unlocked, just as he'd said.

On the breakfast table were several open boxes.

"This isn't porridge," sniffed Mommy Bear.

Baby Bear read the labels. "Wheetos, Munch Flakes, and Puffo Pops."

"Sounds all right to me," said Daddy Bear. "Pour away, Baby-o!"

"These Wheetos are too sweet," said Daddy Bear.

"These Munch Flakes are too noisy," said Mommy Bear.

"But these Puffo Pops are just right," said Baby Bear, aiming a spoonful toward Daddy Bear.

The Puffo Pops hit Daddy Bear in the eye. He launched a spoonful of Wheetos. They splattered all over Mommy Bear's best blouse.

Soon cereal was flying left and right, until the floors, the walls, and the ceiling were dripping with brown goo.

Then Baby Bear turned on the radio. "Let's dance!" he squealed.

Mommy and Daddy Bear tangoed on the table. "This table's too slippy," said Daddy Bear.

They did the cha-cha
around the curtains.
    "These curtains are
too rippy," said
Mommy Bear.

"But this sofa's just right,"
squeaked Baby Bear, so they
all jumped on the sofa and
did the bossa nova
until . . .

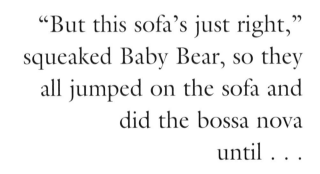

19

they went right through it!

Next the three bears went
upstairs. There were lots of
things to try in the bathroom.
   "This shaving cream's
too creamy," grumbled
Daddy Bear.

"This toothpaste's
too minty," gargled
Mommy Bear.

"But this bubble bath is
just right," cried
Baby Bear from beneath
a mountain of suds.
   "All right, here
we come," said
Mommy Bear.

They had a wonderful time . . .

splashing in the bath.

Once they were clean and the bathroom a mess,
they moved on to the bedroom.

"These pajamas are too tight," said Daddy Bear,
bursting the buttons.

"This mattress is too lumpy," said Mommy
Bear, bouncing up and down.

"But these pillows are just right,"
said Baby Bear. "Just right for a
pillow fight."

Baby Bear biffed Mommy Bear. Mommy Bear whacked Daddy Bear. Pillows split open, filling the room with clouds of feathers. Suddenly Daddy Bear stopped. "Listen!" he said. "I hear someone."

Quietly, the three bears crept downstairs.

Goldilocks was in the kitchen. Daddy Bear, Mommy Bear, and Baby Bear gleefully spied on her from behind the door.

Goldilocks gasped when she saw the cereal splattered all over the walls.

Her eyes grew large when she
saw the ripped curtains and the
gigantic hole in the sofa.

She whistled when
she saw the flooded
bathroom decorated
with shaving foam
and toothpaste.

Next Goldilocks went into the bedroom.
She stared openmouthed at the broken
bed covered with feathers. Then the three
bears jumped out from behind the door.

"Surprise!" they shouted.
   "We thought *we'd* pay *you* a visit,"
said Mommy Bear.
      Goldilocks looked at them,
         then back at the room . . .

and to the bears' astonishment, she threw back her head and laughed until her hair shook like golden springs.

"What's so funny?" asked Mommy Bear.

"Aren't you mad at what we've done?" added Daddy Bear.

"This isn't my house," giggled Goldilocks.

"But it must be," said Baby Bear. "I saw you go in."

"Oh that," said Goldilocks. "The door was open, so I thought I'd look around. I'm always sneaking into other people's houses. I only came back because I left my teddy bear behind."

"Then if it's not your house, *whose house is it*?" asked Daddy Bear.
"Oh, help!" squeaked Baby Bear, looking out of the window . . .

WHERE THERE'S A BEAR, THERE'S TROUBLE!

by Michael Catchpool
pictures by Vanessa Cabban

One brown bear saw
one yellow bee.
And one yellow bee
saw one brown bear.

One brown bear thought,
"Where there's a bee there's honey . . .
sticky honey, yummy honey, drippy honey,
gummy honey. I'll follow this bee as quietly
as can be."

One yellow bee thought,
"Where there's a bear there's trouble.
I'll buzz off home as quickly as can be."
So one yellow bee buzzed off over
the stone wall . . .

followed by one brown bear, as
quietly as could be on his
softest tip-toes.

Buzz! Buzz! Growl! Growl! Shh!

Two greedy geese spotted one tip-toeing bear.
"Ah-ha," they thought. "Where there's a bear
there are berries . . . ripe berries,
juicy berries, plump berries, squishy berries.
Let's follow that bear as quietly as can be."

So two greedy geese followed one
brown bear, and one brown bear
followed one yellow bee . . .

Buzz! Buzz! Growl! Growl! Honk! Honk! Shh!

all going along as quietly as can be.

Three shy mice spied two flapping geese.
"Ah-ha," they thought, "where there
are geese, there's corn . . .

yellow corn, yummy corn, delicious corn, tasty corn. Let's follow those geese as quietly as can be."

Buzz! Buzz! Growl! Growl! Honk! Honk! Squeak! Squeak! Shh!

So one yellow bee buzzed over the bramble bush,
and one brown bear followed one yellow bee, and
two greedy geese followed one brown bear, and
three shy mice followed two greedy geese,
all going along as quietly as could be!

Then one yellow bee buzzed
right into its nest . . .

and one hundred yellow
bees buzzed out!

One brown bear saw one hundred yellow bees, and one hundred yellow bees saw one brown bear.

"Help!" growled one brown bear.
"Where there's a swarm
there must be

TROUBLE!

I'll run back home
as quickly as can be."
And off he raced, back through the
prickly bramble bush.

"Help!" squawked the two greedy geese.
"The bear is after us!"
And off they flapped
across the muddy field.

"Help!" squeaked the three shy mice.
"The geese are after us!"
And off they scrabbled through
a crack in the stone wall, until . . .

Growl! Ouch! Squawk! Hiss!

Squeak! Eek!

BOUNCE . . .

WOBBLE . . .

CRASH!

One brown bear landed on two greedy geese,
and two greedy geese landed
on three shy mice.

And one yellow bee thought,
"I knew there'd be trouble!"

Who's Been Eating My Porridge?

by M. Christina Butler

pictures by

Daniel Howarth

Little Bear never ate his porridge.

"All little bears eat porridge," said Mommy Bear. "It makes them big and strong."

But Little Bear shook his head. "No porridge," he said. "No porridge."

"Then I'll give it to Old Scary Bear,
who lives in the woods," said Mommy Bear.
   And Little Bear watched as Mommy Bear
took the porridge outside and left it on an
old tree stump.

That day while Mommy and Daddy Bear
gathered honey from the bees, Little Bear
climbed trees and watched out for
Old Scary Bear.

On the way home, Daddy Bear said,
"Did you see Old Scary Bear?"
   "No," replied Little Bear with his nose
in the air, "because there is no Old Scary Bear!"
   "Well, someone has eaten your porridge,"
said Mommy Bear when they got back
to the bear den.

The next morning, Daddy Bear put some
honey on Little Bear's porridge, but Little
Bear still would not eat it.

"I don't like porridge. It's horrible!"
he cried.

So Daddy Bear
took it outside
and left it on the
tree stump for
Old Scary Bear.

That day, Grandma and Grandpa Bear came to stay and they all went out to pick berries.

"I hear you don't eat your porridge, Little Bear," said Grandpa Bear as they walked home. "It's no wonder Old Scary Bear has been around. Old Scary Bear loves porridge."

When they arrived back at the
bear den, Little Bear ran over to
the tree stump and found that his
porridge bowl was empty again!

The next morning, Grandma Bear
put some honey and berries on
Little Bear's porridge, but Little Bear
held his nose and closed his eyes.

"No porridge!" he cried. "I hate
porridge!"

And so Grandpa Bear took the porridge
outside again for Old Scary Bear.

That day, Little Bear's aunt and uncle and his two cousins came for a visit.

While the grown-up bears gathered nuts in the woods, Little Bear and his cousins played Old Scary Bear games among the trees.

On the way home, Little Bear was very quiet and wouldn't speak to anyone.

"I bet he's tired," said Daddy Bear.

At dinnertime, Little Bear wasn't feeling
hungry. Daddy Bear took him upstairs
and tucked him into bed.

That night Little Bear had a bad dream.
Old Scary Bear was chasing him through
the woods.

"I want your porridge," he growled.
"It makes me big and strong!"

Little Bear ran and ran with his porridge . . .
over the fields where the berries grow . . .
through the woods where the nuts
grow, and past the hives where the
bees make honey . . .

until he came
to the old tree stump.
"You're not getting
my porridge!" he shouted
to Old Scary Bear, and he
sat down and ate up all
his porridge – every bit.

And then he woke up.

The next morning at breakfast, Little
Bear ate a bowl of porridge with
honey...

and then he had
a second helping
with nuts and
berries.

All day long Little Bear was very busy. He
helped Grandma Bear and Mommy Bear make
berries into jam and put honey into jars.

Then he went to help Grandpa Bear and Daddy Bear. As they were storing the nuts, Daddy Bear said suddenly, "What's that noise?"

All the bears listened carefully and then they looked outside.

There in front of the bear den were lots of little animals all shouting, "Where's our porridge? Where's our porridge?"

"So *that's* who Old Scary Bear is!" cried Little Bear with a giggle.

And from that day to this one, every morning when Little Bear finishes eating his porridge, he takes another bowl of porridge outside for *Old Scary Bear*. And it always gets eaten!

Big Bear
Little Bear

DAVID BEDFORD AND JANE CHAPMAN

One bright cold morning Little Bear helped
Mother Bear scoop snow out of their den.
"This will make more room for you to play,"
said Mother Bear. "You're getting bigger now."

"I want to be as big as you when I'm grown up," said Little Bear. He stretched up his arms and made himself as big as he could.

Mother Bear stretched to the sky.
"You'll have to eat and eat to be
as big as I am," she said.
"When I'm big, I'll wrestle you
in the snow," said Little Bear.
Wrestling in the snow was
his favorite game.

"You're not big enough to wrestle me yet,"
said Mother Bear, laughing.
   She rolled Little Bear over and over in
the soft snow and Little Bear giggled.

Little Bear shook the snow from his fur.
  "When I'm grown up I want to run as
fast as you, Mommy," he said.
  "You'll have to practice if you want to
be as fast as I am," said Mother Bear.

Little Bear darted away and
ran as fast as he could . . .

but his mother soon caught up with him.

"Run faster!" she called.

"I can't," said Little Bear. "I'm not grown up yet."

"I'll show you what it's like to be grown up," said Mother Bear. "Climb onto my shoulders!" When Little Bear stood on his mother's shoulders he could see to the end of the world, and when he reached up his hands he could nearly touch the sky. "Now you *are* big," said Mother Bear.

"Let's run," cried Mother Bear, and she ran faster and faster.

Little Bear felt the wind rushing against his face and blowing his ears back.

"This is how I'll run when I'm grown up," he shouted.

Suddenly, Mother Bear leapt into the air.
Little Bear saw the world rushing under him.
"I'm flying like a bird," he shouted.
Then he saw where they were going to land . . .

SPLASH!

Mother Bear dove into the cold water and swam along with Little Bear on her back.

"This is how you'll swim when you're grown up," she said.

Little Bear watched his mother carefully so he would know what to do next time.

"I'll soon be able to swim like that," he told himself.

Mother Bear climbed out of the water with Little Bear still clinging tightly to her back.

"Will I *really* be as big as you when I'm grown up?" asked Little Bear.

"Yes you will," said his mother— "but I don't want you to grow up yet."

"Why not?" asked Little Bear.

"You won't be able to sit on my shoulders when you're grown up," said Mother Bear, as she carried Little Bear back to their snow den.

Little Bear was tired after wrestling,
running, flying, and swimming.
"You can still cuddle me when
I'm grown up," he said, sleepily.
"But Mommy," he whispered,
"I don't want to grow up yet."

"That's good," said Mother Bear,
holding him close, "because . . .

you're perfect just the way
you are."

Little Bear snuggled into his
mother's soft fur, and they
went to sleep together in
their cozy den in the snow.

When will it be Spring?

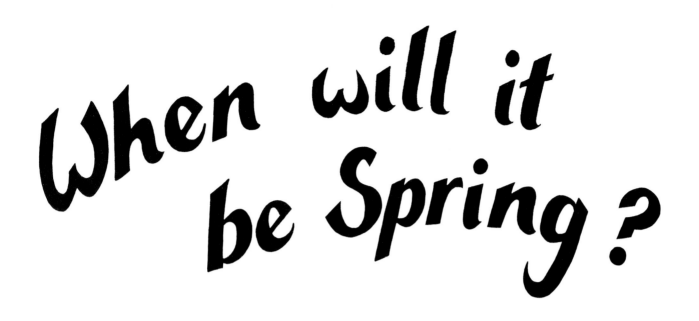

CATHERINE WALTERS

"Come inside, Alfie," said Mother Bear. "It's time to sleep, and when you wake up it will be spring."

"When will it be spring?" asked Alfie. "And how will I know when it's here?"

Mother Bear replied, "When the butterflies float by looking for new flowers, then it will be spring."

So Alfie snuggled down
to sleep . . .

but when he woke up
Alfie could not tell if spring had
come or not. He tiptoed across the floor
of the cave, rubbed his bleary
eyes, and saw . . .

BUTTERFLIES!

"It's spring! It's spring!" cried Alfie.
"Wake up, Mother! I see a big gray butterfly
and lots of little white ones!"

But when Mother Bear came out, she
could only see the soft fall of new snow.

"Winter has hardly begun," she said.
"Go back to sleep, Alfie."

"But when *will* it be spring?" Alfie
wanted to know.

And Mother Bear mumbled sleepily,
"When the swallows arrive, and there are birds
in every tree. *Then* it will be spring."

Then Alfie curled up
again to sleep . . .

. . . and when he woke
he was sure it must
be time for spring.

He crept across the floor,
peered outside,
and saw . . .

BIRDS IN THE TREES!

"Mother Bear, wake up!" squealed Alfie. "Spring is here! The swallows have come. And they are singing in the trees."

But Mother Bear could only see icicles and
hear the wind whistling in the bare branches.
"You're dreaming, Alfie," she said.
"Now go back to sleep."
"But Mother," said Alfie,
"when *will* it be spring?"
And Mother Bear,
already half asleep, grunted,
"When the sun is bright
and the air is warm.
Then it will be spring."

So Alfie burrowed down in his bed again . . .

. . . and when he woke, he was quite sure
spring was here. He padded across the floor,
looked out, and saw . . .

A BRIGHT SUN!

"Mother, you've overslept!"
cried Alfie. "Wake up! Spring is here.
The sun's shining and it's getting warm!"

But Mother Bear could only
see the hunters' fires and quickly
hustled her cub away.

  "Now go to sleep!" she said.
"I will tell you when
spring is here."

So Alfie slept and dreamed of butterflies, birds, and sunshine until something icy touched his nose! A tiny stream of water was trickling through the cave.

Alfie shook his mother awake and she growled, "For the very last time, Alfie, it is *not* spring."

But Alfie patted her
hopefully until she got up,
stomped through
the doorway,

and saw . . .

SPRING!

Mother Bear rubbed her eyes and blinked in the warm, bright light.

"Spring is here after all," she said with a smile. "But *where* is Alfie?"

I'll Always Love You

by
Paeony Lewis

pictures by
Penny Ives

One morning Alex woke up early
and ran downstairs to the kitchen.
  "I'll make Mom some toast and
honey for breakfast," he said.
"She'll like that."

Alex reached for the honey bowl and . . .

CRASH!

His mom's favorite bowl was now nine pieces of sticky china.

Alex hadn't *meant* to break it. What would she say?

Alex's mom was doing her morning exercises.
"Hello, Alex," she said. "Did I hear something break?"
"Mom, will you only love me if I'm good?" asked Alex.

"I'll always love you," said his mom, and she smiled.

"Even when I've done something that *isn't* good?" asked Alex.

"I'll still love you," said his mom. "Honest."

"What if I have a pillow fight with Joey Bear
and all the feathers burst out?
Will you still love me?"

"I'll always love you. Though you must
pick up all the feathers."

"What if I spill my new paints on Baby Pog
and she turns green, red, and blue?
Will you still love me?"

"I'll always love you. Though you
will have to give her a bath."

"What if I forget to close the fridge
door and Baby Pog pulls everything out?
Will you still love me?"

"I'll always love you. Though there
won't be any food for dinner."

"What if I pour Grandma Bear's lumpy oatmeal all over my head? Will you still love me?"

"I'll always love you. Though you will
have to eat another bowl of oatmeal.
Now, why are you being such a silly bear
this morning?"

For a few moments Alex didn't say anything.
Then he whispered, "What if I break your
favorite honey bowl? Will you still love me?"
"You know I'll always love you,"
said his mom. "Come on, Alex.
It must be time for breakfast."

And off they went to the kitchen.

"Oh no!" cried his mom when she saw the nine pieces of sticky china. "That was my favorite bowl, Alex."

"Sorry," said Alex. Two tears ran down his face.
"You said you would still love me. I love *you*."

"Of course I love you," said
Alex's mom, hugging him.

"Hey, I've got an idea!"
shouted Alex, wriggling
from her arms.
"What is it?" she asked.
"It's a surprise," Alex
said and he ran off
to his bedroom.

He looked in his toy box . . .

and he looked under his table.
At last he found what he wanted.

He got out his new paints, poured
some water into a jelly jar, and
swirled his paintbrush around.

A little while later, Alex came downstairs again.
"Here you are, Mom," he said. "But be careful,
the paint's still wet."
"I'll be *very* careful," said his mom, smiling.
"Because this is going to be my new
favorite honey bowl!"